THE QUINN FAMILY ADVENTURES

The Mayan Ruins

By Erin Ritch

Published by

No Wyverns Publishing
PO Box 32
Dorena, OR 97434
http://ErinRitch.com/
Erin@NoWyverns.com

ISBN: 1519146981
ISBN-13: 978-1519146984

CONTENTS

CHAPTER ONE

13-year-old Dawn Quinn jumped out of her family's station wagon and into Guatemala's warm March heat. The famous archaeologist and Dawn's father, Stanley Quinn, got out from the driver's seat of the car. Alana Quinn, Dawn's mother who was also an archaeologist, stood from the air-conditioned station wagon.

A tall man came up to the Quinn family from across the street and greeted them cheerily. "There you three are! Sure took your time getting here."

"We wanted to see Mexico's beauty, Wayne. There's a lot to see!" Stanley Quinn laughed, shaking his hand.

Wayne smiled at Mrs. Quinn. "Hi Alana, where's Dawn?"

Mrs. Quinn returned the smile and pointed to the other side of the station wagon.

Dawn was carefully examining a curious bird that had neared her. Wayne snuck up on the distracted girl and shouted, "Hi Dawn!"

The strange little bird squawked and ran away. Dawn jumped and turned around.

"Thanks, a lot!" she laughed.

"I see you're still bird crazy," Wayne teased.

"Bird crazy? The term is 'bird watching' Wayne. Bird watching," Dawn corrected seriously.

Wayne smiled and nodded. He helped Mr. Quinn open the station wagon's large trunk. Dawn walked up to her mother and looked around. They were in the heart of the city of Guatemala, in the country of Guatemala. The city of Guatemala was the capital of the beautiful, tropical country. The Quinn family had been sent by the Blau Archaeology

Company to survey and search the wild jungles for lost Mayan ruins. Wayne Curtis, Stanley Quinn's partner, was joining in on the trip to northern Guatemala.

Mayan ruins had already been found years ago in central Guatemala. The Quinn family had been sent to search the northern, more remote area of the country. They were warned that they would have to travel on foot, for there were no decent roads that cut through the rainforests of northern Guatemala. The Quinn family still accepted the challenge - they loved adventures and spending time together solving problems.

Their hotel was located in an area of the city that was covered with towering trees and vines that hung down into the streets. Citizens of Guatemala walked along the cracked sidewalks.

Dawn looked over at her mother. "When will we be able to leave on the expedition?"

"It could be weeks, dear. We still have to hire our guides and the men to carry our survey equipment."

Dawn sighed and watched as her father and Wayne continued to unload their research equipment. Weeks sounded like a long time.

She looked around for any other birds she could study. Ever since she was bitten on the nose by a parrot years ago, Dawn had been fascinated by the winged creatures. She focused her binoculars and searched through the treetops swiftly. A bird with brightly colored feathers caught her sharp eyes.

"What! What is that bird?" Dawn shouted.

Wayne looked up to the trees where Dawn was pointing. "That? Oh, that's Guatemala's national bird, or whatever they call it. It's a Quetzal, I believe," he explained.

"A Quetzal…" Dawn whispered, fascinated by the bird's colorful wings.

Mrs. Quinn called to Dawn from a few yards away. "Time to go to the hotel! I'm sure there are plenty of birds for you to study some other time."

"Coming!" Dawn yelled, backing up slowly but still pointing the binoculars towards the Quetzal.

Dawn suddenly bumped into a pedestrian walking along the sidewalk in front of the hotel. Dawn turned and bumped against the building, dropping her binoculars. One of the binocular lenses broke into several pieces, scattering across the sidewalk.

The girl that Dawn had bumped into ran up to her. Dawn knelt down to the sidewalk and picked up her broken binoculars. She sighed in disappointment. Those binoculars were a present from a famous archaeologist, specially made just for Dawn.

"I am so sorry," the girl apologized, her voice thick with a Spanish accent.

Dawn looked up at the young girl. She tried not to look upset and said, "That's alright, it was my fault." Dawn scooped the broken binoculars up in her hand.

The girl grabbed the binoculars. "I will have them fixed for you!"

Dawn opened her mouth to explain they couldn't be fixed but the girl sprinted off and disappeared. She shrugged her shoulders and joined her mom, who was waiting in the hotel lobby.

"What happened?" Mrs. Quinn asked, observing her daughter looked sad.

Dawn quickly explained what had just happened.

"We'll get you a new pair of binoculars, don't worry," Mrs. Quinn assured.

Dawn nodded. She had just got used to those binoculars and now they were gone. Dawn trudged up to her family's hotel room and entered. Wayne and Mr. Quinn chattered away, discussing what equipment would be suitable for the journey.

Dawn jumped on her bed and rummaged

through her backpack. She pulled out a map of Guatemala and looked at the unpopulated area they were sent to search. Wayne threw a measuring stick at Dawn.

"How about some help?" he chuckled.

Dawn nodded, always ready to tinker with her father's survey equipment.

Mr. Quinn looked down at her. "What do you think we need the most? We can't bring it all."

Dawn scratched her auburn hair in thought. She rattled out a list of what was definitely needed.

"She's right. With that amount of equipment, three men could easily carry it," Wayne agreed.

Mr. Quinn grabbed his hat. "We'll go into town and hire some help. Wayne, why don't you arrange for the guides. Two will do fine."

Dawn jumped up from the ground and followed her parents out the hotel room door.

She ran down the steps and outside, hoping to get a faraway glimpse of the Quetzal, but the bird was gone. Dawn sighed and followed her parents down the sidewalk.

.

CHAPTER TWO

The Quinn family left the employment office. They had hired three men to carry all the necessary equipment then returned to their hotel, exhausted from the long day. When they reached their hotel room, Dawn grabbed the extra pair of binoculars that were lying on the bed. She rushed outside to the small patio and searched the trees for birds. None were found. Dawn mumbled to herself that if she had her old binoculars, she could find the Quetzal.

Suddenly, Wayne burst into the crowded room. "Hey! I've got some great news!"

"Great," Mrs. Quinn replied, flipping through a notebook.

Wayne stumbled over to Dawn who was watching the confusion. "I have some great news, Dawn!"

"Really? What is it?" Dawn replied politely, always ready to listen to her friends.

"I've spoken to the guides and they told me we can leave tomorrow morning!" Wayne whispered.

Dawn's eyes popped open. "Tomorrow?"

Wayne winked. "I'll let you tell them."

Dawn grinned and nodded.

"Well, I better get going, pretty tired," Wayne announced loudly, nearing the door.

Mrs. Quinn looked up from her notebook. "But what was your great news?"

"Oh, nothing much. See you tomorrow morning!" Wayne laughed, closing the door.

Mr. and Mrs. Quinn looked over at Dawn. "Okay, Dawn. What's the secret?" Mrs. Quinn asked, smiling.

"We can leave tomorrow!" Dawn

exclaimed.

"Huh? Leave for what?" Mr. Quinn asked, confused.

"Tomorrow? Leave for the expedition, tomorrow?" Mrs. Quinn screamed.

"This calls for a celebration!" Mr. Quinn laughed.

Mrs. Quinn and Dawn chattered away. They left the hotel happily and entered the restaurant across the cobblestone street.

———————————

Several hours later, after a long dinner that Wayne joined as well, the group entered the lobby of their hotel. The girl who had previously bumped into Dawn ran up from the shadows. She handed Dawn her binoculars and smiled.

"Here they are. I had them fixed for you," the girl announced.

Dawn examined her once broken

binoculars. The lenses were perfectly installed and the binoculars shone from being polished.

"They look better than they ever have!" Dawn gasped. "Thank you so much!"

The girl grinned, obviously pleased.

Dawn searched through her purse. "I'll gladly pay you for the repairs."

The girl shook her head violently. "No, no, no. I will not take any money for breaking your binoculars."

Dawn smiled and awkwardly cleared her throat. The girl looked at her expectantly so Dawn decided to introduce herself.

"My name is Dawn Quinn and I'm here with my parents for an expedition in search of Mayan ruins," she explained.

"I know, your pictures are in the newspaper," the girl replied.

Dawn's jaw dropped open. "Really? Is it a good picture of me?" she asked.

The girl giggled. "Oh yes, very good! My name is Juanita, I am glad to meet you. Although I wish we hadn't met with me breaking your binoculars," Juanita mumbled.

"It was totally my fault, Juan...Juan..." Dawn said, stumbling over the pronunciation of Juanita's name.

Juanita smiled. "You may call me Juany, everyone else does."

Dawn nodded and asked Juany a few questions on Guatemala. Juany admitted that the northern region, where the Quinn's were to investigate, was very remote.

After a brief silence, Juany spoke up shyly. "Uh...I would like to ask you something if I may."

Dawn nodded.

"Can I come with you and your parents on the expedition?"

Dawn blinked. "You want to come with us?" she asked.

"Yes, I would like to. I love history and I read about it all the time. I would love to come along…" Juany begged, her voice trailing off.

Dawn tried to think if there were any problems with this. She realized it wasn't really her decision. After all, it was her parents who were the archaeologists. Dawn just came along because she enjoyed it all.

She looked over at her parents who had been patiently waiting. "I don't see why you couldn't, but I need to ask my parents. Excuse me," Dawn explained.

Mrs. Quinn smiled at Dawn. "Who is that?"

Dawn quickly explained, adding that the girl wanted to join them on their expedition.

"Huh? But we barely know who she is," Mr. Quinn whispered so Juany wouldn't hear.

Mrs. Quinn looked over at the sweet girl. "Oh, it wouldn't hurt to let her tag along," she whispered back.

"Mom's right. And she could be a great translator and she knows a lot about history," Dawn added.

Mrs. Quinn and Dawn looked over at Mr. Quinn. He shrugged his shoulders and sighed, "I guess I'm outnumbered. She can come along if it's okay with her guardians."

"Yes!" Dawn shouted, triumphantly skipping back to Juany. "They said it's fine with them, as long as your parents or guardians say you can come."

"Oh, they'll let me come. Our house is so crowded, with me leaving it will give them a little more room," Juany laughed.

Dawn explained to Juany that they would be leaving early the next morning so she should be at the hotel by 6:00 a.m. Juany left the hotel happily and Dawn joined her exhausted parents. The Quinn family immediately went to bed, realizing that 5:00 in the morning came awfully fast.

CHAPTER THREE

5:45 the next morning, there was a gentle knock at the Quinn's hotel room door. Dawn, pulling her hair back into a braid, ran up to the door and opened it.

Juany shyly smiled at her. "Hi. I'm not too early, am I?" she asked, entering the room after being let in by Dawn.

"Not at all. The earlier the better I always say," Dawn laughed. She quickly introduced Juany to her parents.

"We're happy to have you along, Juanita," Mrs. Quinn welcomed.

"Yeah, I hope you like trudging through rainforests," Mr. Quinn added.

"Yes, I do!" Juany answered.

After telling Mr. and Mrs. Quinn where they were going, Juany and Dawn ran down to the lobby to get their complimentary breakfast offered by the hotel.

As Dawn grabbed a warm roll, Juany mumbled through a full mouth, "Have you heard about the northern region's volcano that is getting ready to blow?"

Dawn snapped around. "Um, what?"

"Well, there's a famous volcano chain starting from Mexico and goes all the way to El Salvador. Most of them are dormant but have been recently rumbling way down where it counts," Juany replied.

"Is it alright to go into the northern region? I mean, if the volcano is going to blow..." Dawn asked.

"I think it will be fine. The volcanoes are far away from any towns or cities. And they always warn when they are near exploding, like with smoke and ash," Juany explained.

Dawn suddenly remembered breakfast for her parents. She grabbed a few more rolls and balanced several cups of coffee. As Dawn stumbled up the stairs to her room, Wayne burst down the steps. Dawn barely kept the coffee from spilling all over her.

"Hey, sorry! Gotta get my complimentary breakfast before they close it up!" Wayne yelled, running to the lobby. Soon after, he ran back up with a sweet roll in his mouth.

"Hi! Who are you?" Wayne asked of Juany in his cheerful way.

"I am Juanita, but you may call me Juany," she replied shyly.

"Juany, huh? Sounds like a coffee brand!" Wayne teased.

Juany politely smiled and nodded.

"Wayne!" Dawn snapped.

Wayne choked down his food and sped off to his room. Juany opened the hotel room door and Dawn handed her parents their breakfast. Mrs. Quinn rushed the girls out of the hotel room as Mr. Quinn began to lock the door.

Mrs. Quinn handed Dawn her backpack. "Oh dear, 6:15...we're late," Mrs. Quinn muttered.

As they entered the busy hotel lobby, they found the two guides talking with Wayne.

"We'll be able to drive about thirty miles until we get to the lowlands region. But from there on it's on foot," Wayne explained.

The group exited the hotel and walked up to the rugged van. Juany tightened her backpack. Dawn grabbed her binoculars and looked up to that familiar tree. In the darkness of morning, she couldn't tell if the Quetzal was up in the tree or not.

"Come on, Dawn," Mrs. Quinn urged.

Dawn jumped into the back of the van and they drove off, packed with passengers and equipment.

Through the noise of the old van, Juany asked Dawn a question. "Who finances your expedition trips?"

"A man named Eniac Blau. He used to be a famous archaeologist until he died from a strange disease out here in Guatemala. He found one of the first Mayan ruins here and got big money for it. He died very rich about ten years ago. And you know what the strange thing is? As he was dying, he kept mumbling the words *Caine... Caine...* No one has the foggiest idea what he was talking about. I think he was trying to tell everyone he was insane. See? *Caine* and *insane* sound alike. Also, doesn't *Eniac* sound like *maniac*? It all makes sense if you look at it like that," Dawn gossiped.

Mrs. Quinn, who had been listening to the whole conversation, turned around. "He must have been mumbling a name, not admitting he was insane. Who admits they're insane?"

"Someone who is insane does, I guess," Dawn giggled.

Mrs. Quinn smiled and went back to her notes.

"So, to finish my story. In Eniac's honor, the Blau Archeology Company was established and uses his fortune to run it," Dawn added.

"That's interesting, especially about those mysterious words he was mumbling," Juany admitted.

Dawn turned to peer out the window. They were speeding down an old road, passing huge trees and thick plants. An animal's eyes stared back at the speeding vehicle.

"What kind of animals are out here in the northern region?" Dawn asked Juany warily.

"There are snakes, but you just steer clear of them. There are also jaguars, monkeys, and parrots," Juany answered.

"Parrots? Perfect!" Dawn gasped, straightening in her seat.

Twenty minutes later, the beat up van couldn't go any farther on the rough road. The guides jumped out and began loading the equipment. Mr. and Mrs. Quinn checked the map and spoke with Wayne about last minute issues, while Juany and Dawn filled their backpacks with emergency water. Dawn and Juany were handed a few other supplies such as a flashlight, rope, and matches.

Dawn heaved the heavy backpack onto her shoulder. "Whoa! I hope I can carry this," she panted.

"Why don't you leave your binoculars behind? Those are pretty heavy," Mrs. Quinn suggested with a smile.

"My binoculars? I think I'll keep them with me," Dawn replied stubbornly.

Once the guides were ready, they joined the others in front of the van. The group began their journey, carefully looking around, wondering what they will find in the wild jungle.

CHAPTER FOUR

Dawn wiped the perspiration dripping from her head. The humid air deep in the rainforest made the trip quite difficult. Juany stumbled over to Dawn.

"How's it going?" she asked, swiping a mosquito from her leg.

Dawn focused the binoculars around the treetops. "I'm hot, but I've been able to find some fascinating species of birds."

"Girls, we need to keep moving," Mrs. Quinn called from up ahead. They had been walking for hours but had a long way to go.

The girls raced to catch up to the group. Dawn stopped to untwist a vine that had caught around her binoculars.

Juany looked back and yelled to the

group, "We'll catch up with you in a second!"

"Don't go far!" Mr. Quinn yelled back.

Juany ran back to Dawn, who was completely tangled in vines. She grunted and made a hard yank on one of the vines. A loud squawk rang out from the treetops from where the vine was dangling. Dawn gasped and looked right up into the eyes of a Quetzal. She fumbled with her binoculars quickly. Suddenly, the Quetzal flew away and Dawn ran after it.

"Dawn! We can't go so far from the group!" Juany warned.

"We won't! Come on!" Dawn yelled from the distance.

Juany caught up with Dawn, who was down on one knee, focusing her binoculars on the Quetzal. The beautiful bird stared down at the girls, ruffling its colorful feathers. As though tired of being admired, the Quetzal flew off once more. The girls followed the bird, deeper and deeper into the rainforest.

Just as Dawn was nearing the Quetzal, the bird flew straight up into the air and far, far away. Dawn and Juany let out a disappointed sigh at the same time. They looked around the small clearing of grass in the middle of the thick rainforest where they had stopped.

"Well, let's go back," Dawn muttered, irritated on losing the bird.

"But which way?" Juany asked.

Dawn scratched her head. "You don't know?"

Juany shook her head.

Dawn called out for the expedition party. Juany joined in the calling. Their answer was only the sound of high pitched bugs and the rustle of leaves as animals fled from the girls' shouts.

"Oh, this is great. We are lost in a rainforest, filled with who-knows-what and we probably won't live through the night," Dawn panicked, dropping her backpack to the ground.

"Don't give up hope. Let's just start walking… in this direction," Juany suggested, pointing to the right.

Dawn nodded. She figured Juany knew more about Guatemalan rainforests than she did. The two girls trampled through the thick foliage. Dawn ducked away from a snake hanging from a tree limb. Juany stopped in her tracks.

"What is it?" Dawn whispered.

"I don't know. I just have a funny feeling," Juany whispered back.

Juany shrugged her shoulders and walked on, closely followed by Dawn. Suddenly, the ground beneath the girls' feet gave away and they were caught in a net, pulling them up into the air. Both girls screamed in unison, their hands and legs slipping through the holes of the net. Dawn quickly sat up and helped Juany, who was hanging upside down.

"What happened?" Juany panted, rubbing her dizzy head.

Dawn peered out of the holes of the net. "This must be some kind of trappers net. You know, to catch beavers and that sort of thing," she suggested.

"I don't think you'll find any beavers around here… but they might want the jaguars," Juany replied.

Dawn pulled at the handmade net. The tightly-woven ropes would hold an elephant. She pulled out her binoculars from her backpack and surveyed the area from their position. The tall rainforest trees blocked any vision into the distance. Juany grabbed a pocket knife from her own backpack. She sawed at the thick ropes vigorously but failed to make any kind of tear in the ropes.

"These are incredible ropes. Unfortunately," Juany sighed.

"Well, I guess nothing can reach us up here," Dawn coughed, trying to find a good side to this predicament.

"Yeah, but we're sitting ducks for snakes," Juany reminded.

Dawn moaned and looked again out through the net. A pair of eyes looked straight back at her. Not an animal's eyes, but the eyes of a human. She gasped and pointed to the bushes. But Juany had seen the eyes, as well.

"Hey! Hey! Get us down!" she shouted.

No response came, but the stare from the mysterious human continued to search the girls.

"Try it in Spanish," Dawn suggested.

Juany chattered away several sentences in Spanish. Still, no response came.

Dawn sighed. "Maybe it's just some animal."

"No, can't be," Juany returned.

"Let me try," Dawn whispered. "Hello there! Can you hear us? My name is Dawn Quinn and this my friend, Juany. What is your name? Hello? What is your name?" Dawn yelled slowly.

The human mumbled something from the

shadows.

"Huh? I cannot hear you. Please… speak… louder…" Dawn asked.

"Caine!" a voice rumbled through the forest. Animals scattered away from their hiding places while birds squawked in terror.

"Whoa. Thank you," Juany chuckled.

"Caine? Your name is Caine?" Dawn called.

"Yes," the voice replied. Suddenly, the pair of eyes disappeared.

"Hey! Where did Caine go?" Juany asked, looking around.

"Here," a voice said behind them.

Dawn twirled around, causing the net to rock. "How about coming out from hiding? We won't hurt you."

The large eyes looked around. A spear stuck out from where Caine was hiding. A young girl, appearing to be around the same age as Juany and Dawn, stepped out from the shadows, dressed in crudely made clothes and carrying the handmade spear. The girl's black hair flew around her face wildly, while her eyes watched the girls carefully.

"Doesn't she ever blink?" Dawn whispered.

Caine carefully circled the net that imprisoned the girls. She poked the spear up at Juany who yelled, "Hey! Careful with that thing." Caine jumped backwards. She gave them a wild look and ran off into the trees.

"Great job. You scared her off!" Dawn moaned.

"Do you think she'll come back?" Juany whispered.

Dawn shook her head. "I think we've given her enough excitement today," she replied, settling into her part of the net. It was going to be a long day.

CHAPTER FIVE

Hours passed slowly for Dawn and Juany as they called for Caine. The wild girl ignored them completely, never coming to talk to them or even staring at them.

"Are you having problems breathing, Juany?" Dawn panted, pulling at the neck of her shirt.

"Yeah, it's all this humidity," Juany replied, clearing her throat.

She grabbed a canteen from her backpack and took a slug of water. Dawn looked around. She wished to see Caine's eyes staring back at her, but didn't. Dawn leaned back on Juany tiredly. Juany sat up suddenly, causing Dawn to fall into the dip of the net.

"What's wrong?" Dawn asked.

"I think I hear Caine," Juany whispered.

Dawn jumped up to her feet and looked around. The slender figure of Caine broke through the thick foliage and fell to the ground of the clearing. A jaguar jumped after her and landed on Caine's outstretched arms.

Dawn gasped. But then the jaguar playfully licked Caine's happy face. She giggled, pushed the animal away and stood up. She looked up at the girls in surprise, as though she had forgotten they were there.

"Where have you been?" Dawn asked.

"River," Caine replied simply.

"River? She probably went swimming. How I'd love to go swimming right now," Juany whined, wiping the sweat from her head.

Caine smirked and expertly climbed the tree that the net was hanging from. She grabbed her spear and sliced the top of the net. The girls went tumbling down to the hard forest floor. Dawn yanked open the net and met the face of the jaguar. The beast roared at her.

Caine jumped down from the tree and looked at the girls. "Why are you here?" she mumbled.

"We don't want to be here, but we're lost," Juany replied.

"Where do you want to go?" Caine asked in a low voice.

"To an expedition party that is out here in the forest. Have you seen them?" Dawn asked anxiously.

Caine cocked her head. "Party? What is this?" she asked.

"Well, it's a group of people that go out looking for old buildings and that sort of thing," Dawn explained.

"No, no one here. Except you," Caine whispered.

Dawn and Juany climbed out from the net. Dawn stretched her cramped muscles.

Juany looked at Dawn and muttered under her breath, "Now what?"

Dawn shrugged her shoulders. "Uh, Caine. How did you get way out here? Are you lost, too?" she asked.

"No, I am not lost," Caine replied.

After a brief silence, she spoke again to the girls. "Come with me, to treehouse."

"Treehouse? You live in a treehouse?" Juany asked.

Caine nodded and led them a few yards through the forest. She stopped at a large, great tree that stretched far into the sky. Motioning for them to stay, Caine climbed the tree expertly. She threw a few vines down to the girls, who looked at them, bewildered.

"Climb!" Caine ordered impatiently.

"I don't know about you, but I cannot climb a vine," Dawn whispered to Juany.

"All I know is I'd rather be up in a treehouse than down here with that jaguar,"

Juany announced and grabbed the vine.

Dawn looked at the jaguar, who stared back at her coldly. She scrambled up the vine and jumped off next to the other girls and looked up to where Caine was pointing. A shrewd treehouse stood hidden behind leaves and vines. Caine climbed up a ladder to the treehouse and helped the girls in. Dawn was reluctant to step on the unsteady floor of the treehouse but crawled on anyway.

The girls sat down next to Caine. She stared at them curiously. Dawn grabbed her binoculars and focused them across the treetops of the rainforest. It was so thick she couldn't see much. Her hope of ever finding the expedition party was starting to fade.

"Find anything?" Juany asked.

Dawn shook her head.

"You look for old buildings, too? Like your party?" Caine asked.

"Yes, why?" Juany replied.

"Old buildings," Caine continued,

pointing over into the west.

"Really? What kind of old buildings?" Dawn asked, now getting excited.

Caine shrugged her shoulders. "Old buildings, high too." Caine acted out something like the shape of a pyramid.

"This must be what we're looking for. Another Mayan ruin!" Dawn squealed.

Juany cheered and the girls hugged each other.

"Can you take us to the old buildings?" Dawn pleaded.

"Yes, but tomorrow. Too late now, dangerous at night," Caine replied, looking out from her treehouse.

Dawn and Juany agreed. Caine jumped up and grabbed a large bowl full of bright red berries. She grabbed a handful and stuck it in her mouth then motioned for the girls to get their share.

Juany shook her head and shuddered

politely. "No, thank you. I don't want to eat strange berries."

Caine grabbed another handful and stuffed them in Juany's mouth, who choked with surprise and tried to spit out the berries. Caine held her hand over Juany's mouth, making it impossible to open it. She finally began chewing. She made a hard swallow and Caine removed her hand.

Juany looked over at Dawn. "They're pretty good. Really good, actually."

Caine grunted and motioned to the berries.

"Go ahead, Dawn," Juany urged.

"I'm waiting to see if you're poisoned..." Dawn replied.

Juany chuckled and shook her head. Caine grabbed a handful of berries and started for Dawn's mouth.

"Wait! I'll do it myself, thanks," Dawn laughed, taking a big bite of berries. The berry juice filled her dry mouth. "These are good!"

Dawn laughed through a full mouth.

Caine smiled, the first one Dawn had seen, and handed the girls a water bucket. After the berries and water had been put away, Caine laid down on the hard floor. Dawn and Juany did the same, comfortable finally in the cool breeze that flowed through the treetops.

Dawn stared at the sunset from her position on the floor. The sun rays filtered through the rainforest softly. Dawn looked over at Juany, who had immediately fallen asleep, her black hair coiled around her head. Dawn turned on her left and looked at Caine. The wild girl laid on her back, arms stretched every which way. She snored loudly, occasionally mumbling in her sleep.

There was something so familiar about her name, but she couldn't remember where she had heard it. Dawn sat up straight in the darkness. What was happening with her parents and the expedition party? Could they have been attacked by wild animals or are they searching in the blackness of the night, looking for the girls? Caine had said herself that the rainforest was no place to be at night. These questions flooded Dawn's mind that night, making it hard to relax. Finally, exhaustion overcame her, and she fell asleep.

CHAPTER SIX

"Caine! Let's take a break!" Juany yelled. It was the next morning and she was trying to catch up to the wild girl walking strongly ahead of her toward the ruins.

The girls had been walking for hours. Caine sighed and stood next to Dawn and Juany as they rested. She leaned on her spear and yawned. The jaguar crawled up next to her.

"What's his name?" Dawn panted.

"*Her* name is Cleo," Caine replied gruffly. The jaguar stared at the girls, interested in the newcomers.

Juany stood up after taking a long drink of water. "How much farther to the old buildings?"

"One," Caine replied.

"One? Oh, she must mean one hour," Dawn translated.

"Let's get moving, I can't wait to get a look at them," Juany grinned, rubbing her hands together.

One hour later, the three girls arrived at a large hill. Cleo had gone home by the order of her mistress.

"We climb this. Takes us to old ruins," Caine announced.

Dawn stared at the intimidating mountain. It made her tired just to look at it.

Juany looked at Dawn with pleading eyes. "Can't we go around it?" she whispered.

"No," Caine replied firmly from halfway up the hill.

Juany cleared her throat and began her climb. She tried to follow in the footsteps left by Caine. Dawn did the same. Several minutes later, Dawn and Juany joined Caine at the top of the hill. On the other side, old ruins of a large city remained. Dawn drew in her breath as she recognized the building style.

"Mayans…" Juany whispered.

Caine motioned for the girls to follow her into the city. Tall trees towered above the ruins, making it impossible to see from a helicopter or plane. A slight breeze blew through the ruins, stirring up dust and loose dirt. Caine stooped down and grabbed an old pot. She handed it to Dawn.

Dawn examined it carefully, trying to decipher the writing on the pot. "I can't make out anything right now. But if I could get it back to some kind of lab…"

Caine looked around the abandoned ruins. "Party here?"

"I wish…" Juany moaned.

"Is there anything else of interest here, Caine?" Dawn asked.

"What kind of interest you look for?" Caine questioned.

"Uh, writings on stone or…old plates, stuff like that," Juany suggested.

Caine stared into the distance as though trying to remember something. "I know where writing are… but cannot go there," she ordered firmly.

"Why?" Dawn asked.

Caine shook her head. "Bad place. Cannot go."

"Is there anything else?" Juany asked.

Caine sighed and nodded. She led them into an old house and pointed to a shelf. Several plates and glasses stood dusty on the shelf. Juany and Dawn examined the utensils. Caine stood at the door of the house nervously.

"What's wrong?" Dawn asked.

Caine shook her head and said nothing.

"I think we better go. Something is bothering Caine," Juany whispered to Dawn.

"You're right, we can come back another time. Who knows? Maybe with the expedition party," Dawn replied.

"Do you really think we're going to find them?" Juany whispered.

"We'll find them soon enough," Dawn answered firmly.

Dawn and Juany joined Caine outside the crumbling house. Juany looked to her right and noticed an odd cave. "Hey look! There's some kind of a cave over there!" she squealed.

"You're right! Let's take a look," Dawn replied, walking forward.

"No!" Caine begged, running in front of them.

"What's bothering you about these ruins? Tell us!" Dawn asked, crossing her arms.

"Ruins don't bother me," Caine replied.

"Is it the cave that bothers you?"

Caine nodded.

"Why? Is there some kind of three-headed monster in there?" Dawn teased.

Caine frowned. "You can go in. But you get the disease," she muttered.

"Huh? Is there a disease flying around in there?" Juany asked, surprised.

"Yes, my father get it," Caine replied.

"Your father? Caine, I beg you, start from the beginning!" Dawn asked, very confused.

Caine sighed. "When I little," she demonstrated the height of a small child. "When I little, my father and I come to these ruins. He see cave, go in, but I wait outside. He come out, face look pink. He say he feel sick. Father fall to ground and I run off, scared. Men come to take father, but never to get me. I hide in forest since. Never go in cave, disease in there."

"How horrible...but who was your father?" Dawn asked.

"His name Eniac Blau. I named after him. Eniac backwards means...Caine," Caine replied sadly.

"Eniac Blau? Now I know where I've heard your name! Remember, Juany? When we were in the truck I was telling you about Eniac Blau? And how he was mumbling the word *Caine*. He was calling for her!" Dawn announced excitedly. She then became quiet. "Caine, I'm so sorry, your father died years ago. But all his money belongs to you!"

"I know he dead. I know I get all his money. But I don't want it. I want to stay in forest," Caine replied loudly. "We must return to treehouse now. We look for party tomorrow."

Juany and Dawn looked at each other, stunned at the story of Caine's past. They ran after her, not wanting to be left in the ruins alone.

CHAPTER SEVEN

The trip back to the treehouse was very silent. Caine stormed through the forest while Dawn and Juany struggled to keep up. When they arrived, Dawn noticed it was almost sunset. The girls climbed the vines and entered the treehouse, exhausted. Caine handed them a bowl of leaves and the bucket of water. The girls hungrily ate the food offered to them with no complaints this time.

"Where do you think we should start looking for the expedition party tomorrow?" Dawn asked Caine when they had finished eating.

Caine was silent for a moment then answered, "Past ruins, there is very high mountain. See everywhere from mountain.

We go there tomorrow."

It was apparent to the girls that Caine was not in a mood to talk. She laid down on the floor and let out a hard sigh. The sun was beginning to hide behind the tall mountains. Juany propped her head on her backpack and slumped to the ground. Dawn did the same. She again wondered about the expedition party and if they would find them tomorrow.

———————————

The three girls got up late the next morning, tired from yesterday's travels. Caine waited at the base of the large tree for Dawn and Juany.

"How far is it to this high mountain?" Juany asked, shaking wood chips from her clothes.

Caine scratched her head with the sharp point of her spear. "Two times as long as yesterday trip," she finally answered.

"What? We might get there at night! Isn't

there another mountain we can go to, that isn't quite as far away?" Dawn pleaded.

"You want to find party, don't you?" Caine asked, raising an eyebrow.

"Of course," Dawn replied sourly.

"Then we must go to the high mountain," Caine declared.

Juany and Dawn reluctantly agreed and followed Caine and Cleo through the rainforest.

"Are you feeling better today, Caine?" Juany asked, stepping over a fallen log.

Caine brushed away a harmless snake with her spear. "Yes. But we must never go to ruins again," she replied.

"Never again? But…" Dawn protested.

"You can go with party. But not with me," Caine insisted.

"If we find my parents and the expedition

party, can I tell them about you?"

Caine rubbed her chin in thought. "If you do, will they give me away?" she asked.

"Well, I really couldn't say. They might. But only because they would think it's the right thing do," Dawn replied.

"Then do not tell them," Caine ordered.

"You don't want to live out here in this forest all your life, do you? All alone?" Juany protested.

"I like forest," Caine replied, petting Cleo.

Juany moaned in exasperation.

"When we find the expedition party and tell them about the ruins, there's going to be hundreds of people out here excavating the ruins. You can't possibly stay hidden," Dawn explained.

Caine kicked leaves up from the ground. "I need to think," she replied.

Dawn nodded and looked at her watch. She was surprised to find they had been walking for over an hour. Several hours later, they reached the ruins. The girls rushed through the ruins quickly and without stopping, as much as Dawn wanted to. They finally rested under a tree, trying to replenish their strength.

"This is unknown forest to me," Caine explained, pointing to the trees that stood ahead of them. Cleo's ears perked up to attention.

"You've never been in this area of the rainforest?" Dawn asked.

"Once, that was when I discover tall mountain. Never come back for years, very dark here," Caine replied seriously.

She stood up, signaling it was time to continue. The girls entered the forest followed by Cleo. Caine stopped several times, taking long inhales of air as though she was smelling for something. Cleo growled continuously.

"This is the creepiest place I have ever seen," Juany whispered.

Dawn could not agree more.

"Not creepy. Unexplored," Caine corrected.

Suddenly, Cleo let out a shrill whine. Caine ran into the bushes where Cleo had disappeared. A loud hiss was let out and Cleo growled loudly. Dawn and Juany could hear Caine shouting and slashing with her spear. Cleo let out one last cry and the rainforest fell silent.

Caine backed out of the bushes. Her face looked concerned. "Come!" she ordered quickly.

The girls asked for no explanation and sprinted after Caine. Juany looked back for Cleo.

"Where's...Cleo?" Dawn panted.

"She… dead…" Caine choked, using her spear to push a path through the thick bushes.

Dawn happened to look down at the ground of the rainforest. Dozens of small snakes slithered toward her silently. She let out a loud scream and chased after Juany and Caine. For a long time, the three girls ran and ran. Stumbling over hidden obstacles in the dark forest, the girls tired quickly.

Finally, it seemed the forest began to thin and clearings became more frequent. A small hill rose before the girls. Once they reached the top, they dropped to the ground, finally able to catch their breath. The strange rainforest stood below them silently.

"All...those...snakes!" Juany gasped.

"They were everywhere. Huge python kill Cleo. Horrible sight." Caine shuddered.

"Poor Cleo..." Dawn whispered.

"I try to stop python..." Caine cried.

"It's not your fault," Juany assured.

Caine nodded and turned her back to the girls. She fiddled with her spear sadly.

Juany looked around from the top of the small hill. A long chain of mountains stretched to the north.

"Dawn, these were the mountains I was telling you about at the hotel. You know, the dormant volcanoes?" Juany explained.

"These mountains? Volcanoes?" Caine asked. "They make loud noises from underground."

"Hm. I guess they aren't so dormant, after all," Dawn said.

"Are you sure we are able to climb those mountains?" Juany asked Caine.

"I climbed, long ago," Caine replied with a shrug.

"Yeah, but I think you're a little more physically fit than we are," Dawn chuckled, looking at Caine's muscular body.

"You can do it. We not have to go to top. Just little way up," Caine assured.

"I think we better get started. It looks like we have a few more hours of daylight left," Juany announced, standing up.

Dawn looked down at the clear grassland on the other side of the small hill. She was glad they didn't have to go through another rainforest to get to the mountain chain.

CHAPTER EIGHT

The three girls set off across the grassland. The tall, prickly grasses struck Dawn in the face but she trudged on. Caine hung her head in thought, obviously sad about losing Cleo. Juany remained silent, taking in the evening's beauty.

Finally, the girls reached the base of a large mountain. Ash flew in the wind, leaving a burnt smell in the air.

"Oh, this is going to be a long climb," Juany moaned, looking up the steep mountain.

Caine silently began climbing the mountain, followed by Dawn and Juany.

Dawn spit ash out of her mouth and

asked, "Why is there all this ash?"

"I think the volcano has been spewing out ash," Juany announced.

"Spewing?" Dawn asked.

"That's what volcanoes do when they're about to blow. They spew out ash," Juany explained further.

"You mean mountain going to blow...soon?" Caine gasped, wide eyed.

"We better hurry, then," Dawn urged, increasing her pace.

Before long, the girls were a quarter of the way up the huge volcano. From their view, they could see all across the rainforest treetops and with Dawn's binoculars, even further.

"See anything?" Juany asked anxiously.

Dawn expertly adjusted the focus on her binoculars. "Not...yet," she answered slowly.

"I see smoke that way," Caine volunteered, pointing to the east.

"Hm… yes! Yes! That's them! They're there! But… something is happening at their camp!" Dawn gasped.

Dawn handed the binoculars to Juany who quickly put them to her eyes. She frowned.

"It must be camp thieves. There's a famous gang here in Guatemala that targets tourists and such," she explained.

"My poor parents. How are we going to help them?" Dawn sighed.

"We scare thieves!" Caine announced.

"How?" Dawn asked.

"You see. Come with me. We go through grasslands until we reach camp. Dark then. At night, we scare them by yelling and screaming and roaring. Works with wild animals, why not work on them?" Caine explained.

"We can try but I have a feeling weapons would be more… forceful," Juany suggested.

"Let's go," Caine ordered, starting back down the volcano.

Dawn put the binoculars away and ran after Caine and Juany.

———————————

The girls ran through the rocky grasslands, darkness approaching faster and faster with each passing minute. The three girls found themselves taking breaks more frequently as they grew tired. Suddenly, they heard a low rumble.

"What was that?" Dawn gasped, standing still. The girls fell silent.

The rumble growled even louder, seeming to make the ground shake. Juany looked around the dark grassland. The grass fluttered in the slight breeze, while the full moon shone down on the girls, leading them in the direction of the camp.

"You don't think it's…the volcanoes…" Dawn whispered.

"Could be," Juany whispered back.

"Then we must go even faster. Come, we are wasting time," Caine said quietly.

Dawn and Juany stumbled after Caine. After several minutes of running, the three girls reached the campsite. The small camp fires danced and cast shadows outside the tents. The wind kicked up suddenly, as though getting ready for a great storm. Muffled sounds came from the largest tent, while the other three tents remained dark and silent.

"They must all be in that large tent," Juany whispered, fear beginning to show on her face.

Dawn took a deep breath and glanced over at Caine. Even she looked a little worried.

"When do we start your plan? And what do we do if it doesn't work?" Dawn asked.

"We start soon. If does not work…we…I don't know. I'll think of it," Caine answered.

Juany wiped the sweat from her forehead. Even at night, the humidity never left. A soft rumble began to build in the distance.

"Uh oh. Why now?" Dawn cried.

"When they come out to investigate, we scream and yell, like I say," Caine whispered.

The rumble grew louder. A half dozen men that Dawn did not recognize as part of the expedition party, ran out from the large tent. They had to be the camp thieves.

"That volcano better not blow. We hit the jackpot with this camp," the tallest of the men shouted to the others.

Caine gave the signal and the girls began screaming. While Dawn and Juany yelled at the confused group, Caine disappeared.

A minute later, Caine's spear flew out from behind the group, stabbing one of them right in the back. The man screamed out and fell to the ground. His partners rushed to his side to see what was wrong, pulling out the spear and helping him up. Dawn and Juany split up, still screaming and yelling in unison with Caine. They began throwing rocks at the group. The thieves backed up, shielding their eyes from rocks. They jumped in a nearby jeep, screaming, "We'll be back!"

The jeep sped off, leaving the camp quiet. Caine jumped into the middle of the camp next to one of the fires. She grabbed her spear from the ground.

"We did it!" Dawn cheered.

RRRRUUUUMMMMBBBBLLLLEEEE

Dawn covered her ears. Smoke filled the air quickly, making it difficult to breathe.

"The volcano!" Juany shouted.

"Let's find everyone and get out of here!" Dawn ordered.

Juany and Dawn ran to the large tent. Caine slipped into the shadows, silently watching. The expedition party was stuffed into the humid tent, hands tied so they could not escape. Dawn freed them and ran to her parents.

"Dawn!" Mrs. Quinn gasped, ripping the gag from her mouth.

"You found us! You'll never guess what's happened to us!" Wayne shouted.

"You'll never guess what's happened to me!" Dawn laughed.

Juany peeked outside the tent and looked around. "We need to leave. The volcanoes are about to blow and those camp thieves will be here any second!"

The group agreed and ran outside. The guides jumped into the other jeep abandoned by the camp thieves, followed by Wayne and Mr. Quinn.

"Come on you two!" Mrs. Quinn called to the girls through the loud wind.

RRRRUUUUUMMMMBBBBLLLLEEE

"Just a second!" Dawn called back.

Mrs. Quinn motioned for them to hurry.

"We have to get Caine. She can't stay here, this is going to be a lava bed soon," Dawn said to Juany.

"I know, but it's going to be hard to get her to leave," Juany agreed.

Dawn ran to the edge of the camp. She could see Caine's familiar eyes blinking at her from behind a bush.

"Caine! You have to leave!" Dawn pleaded.

"But..." Caine whined.

"Caine, listen to us. Those volcanoes are going to blow any second! You can't outrun lava flowing down a mountain!" Juany shouted loudly through the wind.

Caine came out of hiding. She looked into the distance.

"They will take me to orphanage..." she whispered.

"I really don't think they will. I know you don't have any living relatives, but maybe you could stay with us," Dawn suggested.

"You know, this really isn't the place to discuss this!" Juany reminded loudly.

"Juany's right. Come on!" Dawn said firmly, reaching out her hand. Caine took her hand and followed Dawn and Juany to the jeep. The expedition party stared at Caine, amazed.

"Dawn, who is...this?" Mrs. Quinn asked.

"Just a friend, Mom...with a lot of worries," Dawn replied, joining the others in the crowded back seat.

The jeep sped off down a crude road made by the fleeing camp thieves. The waking volcano choked up more smoke and let out a loud roar.

CHAPTER NINE

The small jeep pushed its way through the dense rainforest. Smoke hung in the treetops while animals scattered away, sensing danger.

Caine looked around at the members of the group, who occasionally glanced at her. Dawn gave her an encouraging smile. Caine wondered what these strange people would do with her. She hadn't been with civilization for almost a decade, since she was four years old. Would these people in fancy clothes let her stay with them, or take her back to her rainforest after the volcano had erupted? She wasn't sure which one she wanted more.

The jeep made a sudden turn and stopped on the main road. The group cheered, seeing

their van still parked on the side of the road.
They jumped in, now having more room to
breathe.

Wayne scooted over to where Dawn was
sitting and whispered, "Who's your friend?"

"Leave her alone. I don't think she needs
any of your jokes right now," Dawn sighed,
pushing her dirty hair out of her face.

"Well, you have to tell us sometime! She
looks like she just got out of auditions for the
female version of Tarzan! Haha! I can see it
now...Tarzana, queen of the jungle!" Wayne
laughed loudly.

"Wayne!" Dawn shouted loudly, her face
growing red from anger.

Caine jumped up and put her spear to
Wayne's throat. He grabbed the spear,
sputtering away, trying to move it. Caine held
it firmly, her eyes shining from under her
mass of hair.

"Sorry!" Wayne finally choked.

Caine removed her spear and pushed

Wayne to the ground. She took her place near Dawn and watched him. Wayne scrambled away and sat at the far end of the van.

Dawn smirked and nodded to Caine. Finally, someone who was a match for Wayne.

———————————

The truck stopped in front of their hotel and Dawn had never been so glad to see it. The volcanoes finally let out their fury with fiery red lava exploding through the surface. Residents of the city ran out from their homes and gasped in amazement, assured that the volcano's scorching lava could not reach them.

Dawn mumbled a prayer of thankfulness and sighed.

"That was close," Juany marveled.

Mrs. Quinn nodded and asked, "Now girls, why don't you tell us what has been going on?"

Dawn began telling the story of their adventure so far, with Juany adding any missing details. Caine stayed close to Dawn, amazed by the lights of the city. An hour later, as the girls rested in the Quinn's hotel room, they heard the expedition's side of the story.

They fairly quickly realized the girls were gone. The group called and called, but received no answer. Then they searched around the rainforest but reluctantly had to stop for the night. The next few days were spent looking for the girls. One morning, they found themselves tied up and gagged by the camp thieves. Then Dawn, Juany, and Caine found them.

Dawn admitted to the group that they had found the Mayan ruins. Everyone fell silent as they realized the history of that Mayan city was now covered in burning lava. Wayne went to his room shortly after the conversation. The guides returned to their homes, while Juany and Caine shared a separate room. Juany decided that she would call her parents in the morning.

That night, Caine looked around the dark room. Juany was peacefully sleeping, wrapped in her blankets. The full moon shone through the curtains. A Quetzal sang a beautiful song outside the window, perched on a tree's limb. Caine grabbed several baskets that were filled with soaps and towels and made a crude cage out of them.

She quietly opened the squeaky window and the Quetzal stopped singing. It looked at her strangely. Caine neared the branch and crawled directly under it. She jumped, grabbing the Quetzal quickly. The bird struggled but Caine managed to get it in the cage. The Quetzal surprised Caine by staying quiet in its hiding place under Caine's bed. She fell asleep that night, worried. Worried about what was going to happen to her the next morning.

CHAPTER TEN

The Quinn family met up with Juany and Caine in the lobby after the complimentary breakfast provided by the hotel.

Juany hugged her friend. "I wish I could go with you on all of your adventures. I learned a lot from this trip, a whole lot!" Juany laughed.

"So did I. And I also got a pair of polished binoculars out of it!" Dawn agreed.

Juany silently whispered her farewell to Dawn. She turned to Caine and sighed, "I hope everything works out for you, friend."

Caine gave a slight smile. She looked down at her clothes given to her by Dawn.

"So long…Juany," Caine mumbled.

Juany smiled and said her goodbyes to Mr. and Mrs. Quinn. She waved to her friends as she got in a battered old car, stuffed with children of all ages.

"Caine. Would you excuse us for a moment?" Mrs. Quinn asked politely. Caine nodded and watched the Quinn family walk across the hotel lobby.

"Okay. What's the plan with Caine? Before you answer that, remember that she helped us survive while we were lost and it was her who had the idea that rescued the expedition party," Dawn whispered.

"But Dawn, she's Caine Blau! She needs to be with her relatives. She deserves to have her father's fortune," Mr. Quinn replied.

"She said she doesn't want it!" Dawn insisted.

"Stanley. She's been in the wild for years and years. She can't possibly immediately fit in with a group of rich archaeologists. I think…

I think we need to give her a home. She needs one," Mrs. Quinn whispered.

"You mean adopt her?" Mr. Quinn gasped.

Dawn and Mrs. Quinn nodded at the same time.

"Can we do that? I mean, no one has heard of the missing daughter of Eniac Blau and I'm sure they would like to know!" Mr. Quinn protested.

"Dad! Who knows what will happen to her! What if she's put in an orphanage?" Dawn pleaded.

Stanley Quinn sighed in thought. He finally nodded. "We'll adopt her …but only if that's what she wants."

Dawn and Mrs. Quinn cheered silently. Dawn ran over to Caine with a big smile on her face.

"You tell her. We'll wait in the car," Mrs. Quinn called from the hotel lobby's main door.

Dawn caught her breath. "I have something important to ask you," she finally said.

"Tell me on way to room. I have to get something," Caine replied.

Dawn followed Caine up the steps slowly, trying to find the right words. She decided to just blurt it out. "We want you to be part of our family. What do you think?" she asked.

Caine's eyes opened wide. She smiled and nodded.

"Really? Oh! That's great!" Dawn squealed. "You're sure you're okay about it? Leaving the forest, too?"

"Yes, I am okay about it," Caine replied softly.

"I have to tell you, we travel a lot on our archeology expeditions. I hope you like living on the road," Dawn admitted.

"Living on the road?" Caine questioned.

"Oh, that means traveling a lot," Dawn

explained. She would have many phrases to teach her new sister.

"I like archaeology. Remember, my father liked it, too," Caine said.

The two girls reached the room Caine and Juany had shared. Caine asked Dawn to wait outside the hotel room. Moments later, she returned carrying the cage that held the Quetzal. Dawn gasped in surprise at the beautiful creature. The bird's feathers laid in colorful layers, making it look like a rainbow.

"Caine! Where did you get her?" Dawn whispered, petting the friendly Quetzal.

"She at window last night," Caine explained. She handed the Quetzal to Dawn. "Juany tell me you like birds."

"Since you gave me such a great gift, I want you to pick the name for her," Dawn insisted.

Caine thought about this for a brief moment. "Cleo..." she finally whispered and Dawn agreed it was perfect.

Dawn, Caine, and Cleo left the hotel and climbed into the Quinn's station wagon. Wayne sat in the back seat and choked on his croissant when he saw Cleo.

As the station wagon left Guatemala, Cleo sang a song of happiness.

ABOUT THE AUTHOR

Erin Ritch studied Film at the Vancouver Film School and holds a degree in English Literature. She lives with her husband and daughter on their fledgling farm in rural Oregon. Follow Erin at NoWyverns.com or on Twitter at @Eritch324.

ABOUT THE COVER ILLUSTRATOR

Matt Smith is an illustrator and cartoonist who has lived all over the world with his wife and two cats. You can find his comics at http://SmithvsSmith.com and follow him on Instagram @smithvssmithcomics.

Made in the USA
Coppell, TX
01 September 2021